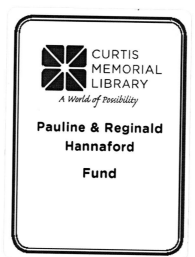

AK Classics
P.O. Box 77203
Charlotte, NC 28271
www.akclassicstories.com
info@akclassicstories.com

Grace Press LLC
1235 East Blvd Suite E PMB 126
Charlotte, NC 28203
www.kathyizard.com

Library of Congress
Published by Grace Press

ISBN: 978-0-9977784-2-7

Illustrations by Evelyn Henson

Design by Rick Daniel

Printed in the U.S.A.

# A GOOD NIGHT FOR MR. COLEMAN

WRITTEN BY Kathy Izard

ILLUSTRATED BY Evelyn Henson

A joint publishing venture

grace press    AK CLASSICS

LEMONADE

YOU CAN DO ANYTHING! REALLY, ANYTHING!

# DEDICATION

For Lauren, Kailey, Emma and Maddie: my four Graces.
And grandparents loved and remembered: Gigi & Poppa,
Lili & Poppy, Granny & Poppop.


For Eugene Coleman and Kat, two real life heroes in this book.
And in thanks to Peggy Hess Greenawalt who asked me
to create this book to inspire children to Do Good.

-Kathy


For Rocky Henson and the family who loved him.

-Evelyn

Today I woke up with a smile because it's my favorite day of the month: Soup Kitchen Sunday! I get to help make tons of sandwiches and loads of soup for people who are hungry.

Mom says we work at the Soup Kitchen to remind us to Believe in Something Bigger than Ourselves. I am not sure what that means. I just know I like helping people and putting on a special purple apron.

When we are at the Soup Kitchen, we call everyone we serve a Neighbor so we can remember to be as nice to them as we are to people who actually live next door to us like Mrs. Cook.

I call Mrs. Cook "Gigi" and she has awesome red glasses with hair that looks like she is wearing clouds. Gigi paints every day in her art studio and she always asks me to paint with her.

I mostly just watch because I am afraid I am not a very good artist. Gigi always shakes her silver hair and tells me You Can Do Anything, Grace! Really, Anything. My name is Grace.

The Neighbors in the Soup Kitchen don't have a home like me or Gigi so they don't have kitchens or bathrooms. They come to the Soup Kitchen every day to eat lunch and even take a shower. But there are no bathtubs or toys.

Mom says serve everyone with a smile and that is easy to do because helping makes me feel all shiny inside. Especially when I help my friend Mr. Coleman.

Mr. Coleman gets all his letters delivered to the Soup Kitchen since he doesn't have a mailbox. When I hand Mr. Coleman his mail he says Why Thank You Miss Grace! I ask him why he doesn't have a home and he says because he lost his job. I ask him Why and he says It's Complicated.

I ask Mom if Mr. Coleman can move in with us since he doesn't have a home but she said No. I ask Why Not and she says It's Complicated. Grownups always say Its Complicated when they don't have the words to explain stuff but I still wish they would try.

I always thought Mr. Coleman and all the Neighbors slept upstairs at the Soup Kitchen so I ask my mom if she would take me to see Mr. Coleman's bed. She looks at me funny and says Nobody Sleeps Here.

But Where is Mr. Coleman's Bed? I ask her. Mom doesn't answer. If he doesn't have his own bed, how does Mr. Coleman ever have a Good Night? I thought.

It scares me to think about Mr. Coleman alone in the dark with no bed and no pillow and no bear like the one I hug at night. He doesn't even have a dog like my Rocky to protect him.

Can't We Do Something About It? I ask my mom. It's Complicated she says. But I keep hearing a little voice that won't go away telling me to do something about it.
So I decided to trust the whisper.

The next day after school, I set up a lemonade stand with a sign that said Let's Build Beds. Lemonade $1. If I sell lemonade every day for a whole year that would have to be enough to get Mr. Coleman his own bed.

I tell Gigi about Mr. Coleman and that he doesn't have a bed or a pillow or a bear or a Rocky.
Gigi says We Must Do Something About That Grace!

Then, Gigi shows me a newspaper article where some grownups are trying to build a whole apartment building for Neighbors who don't have a place to live like Mr. Coleman.

So, I keep selling lemonade and Mom helps me send the money I make to the grownups who are building apartments for Neighbors who don't have homes. And Gigi gives them money, too. I don't know how much but Mom says it was a lot!

And guess what? All those dollars added up and the grownups really did build a building so that Mr. Coleman and lots of Neighbors would have a bed and a pillow in their own homes. I thought Mr. Coleman still needed one more thing to have a Good Night, so I give him my bear, too.

Now Mr. Coleman is no longer a Soup Kitchen Neighbor just a neighbor like Gigi. And he has his own mailbox so I can send him letters and pictures. Because I finally tried painting with Gigi and it turns out I am a pretty good artist. Mr. Coleman even hung some of my paintings on his new bedroom wall.

Sometimes things aren't Complicated. It turns out You Can Do Anything! Really, Anything.
When you Believe in Yourself AND Something Bigger!

## ABOUT THIS STORY AND MR. COLEMAN

A Good Night for Mr. Coleman is based on the true story of Eugene Coleman who was homeless for years before being housed in the Homeless to Homes program developed by the Urban Ministry Center (UMC). In 2012, UMC opened Moore Place, the first permanent supportive housing for chronically homeless men and women in Charlotte, NC. This home for over one hundred, was built by love including the donations of children who had a lemonade stand and sent their dollars to the Urban Ministry Center to help give people a home. Coleman's full story and many more are told in the adult nonfiction book, **The Hundred Story Home**. Coleman still lives and sleeps well in Charlotte.

grace_mr.coleman

## ABOUT THE AUTHOR

Kathy Izard is a consultant, author and speaker who lives and writes in Charlotte, NC. Kathy met Coleman at The Urban Ministry Center when she was the first director of Homeless to Homes and helped lead the effort to build Moore Place. Kathy grew up in El Paso, Texas raised by parents who taught her to believe she could do anything, really, anything. She and her husband, Charlie, have four daughters who all volunteered in a soup kitchen just like Grace. Learn more by visiting:

**www.kathyizard.com** and **www.urbanministrycenter.org**

kathyizardclt

## ABOUT THE ILLUSTRATOR

Evelyn Henson is a Southern artist painting art and gifts for a more brightly decorated life. With a colorful mix of gouache, acrylic, and watercolor, her art is designed to bring sunshine for years to come. She is currently based in Charlotte, NC and you can follow her work through Instagram or by visiting:

**www.evelynhenson.com**

evelyn_henson

# READER'S GUIDE - QUESTIONS FOR DISCUSSION

1. What was your favorite part of this book?

2. Do you have a Neighbor or an adult in your life that encourages you like Mrs. Cook (Gigi) encourages Grace?

3. Grace's parents are not seen in the book. Why do you think that is?

4. Why do you think Grace felt bad that Mr. Coleman did not have a home or a place to sleep?

5. What do you think it would be like to be homeless like Mr. Coleman?

6. Why do you think people are homeless? What are some of the reasons someone might not have the money to pay for an apartment or home?

7. Have you ever seen someone who is homeless? What did you do?

8. Grace said she felt "all shiny inside" when she helped at the soup kitchen. Have you ever helped someone and how did it make you feel?

9. Have you ever not had a good night sleep maybe staying up late at a sleepover? How did it make you feel the next day?

10. Have you ever been really hungry maybe if you forgot your lunch box or money to buy lunch at school? How did you feel?

11. How do you think Grace felt after she gave Mr. Coleman her bear at the end so he could have a good night?

12. Grace said she couldn't ignore the little voice that was telling her to do something about Mr. Coleman. Have you ever heard a little whisper like this and what did you do about it?

13. Where do people in your town or city go for help if they are homeless particularly if there is bad weather like snow?

14. Are there problems in the world you worry about? Do you have ideas about what you could do about it?

15. Grace wanted to do something to help Mr. Coleman have a home. What is a way you can Do Good in the world?

Thank you to Anna Grace Frenzel, Ruthie Hayes, Lilly Hobson, Anne Gibson McBryde, Reese Pham, Graham Scott and Holland Wilkins for creating this Reader's Guide and to Michelle Frenzel for the inspiration.

Thank you also to Meg Robertson, Olivia and Nate Mackel, Ericka, Christian and Sophia Lopez for being beta readers of this story and adding great suggestions.

And thank you Helen Hope Kimbrough and Rick Daniel for the final magic!